THE LIL GIRL WHO WON THE LOTTERY

Malachi Brooks

1

Dedicated to My Daughter "Tay" x

Once upon a time, there lived a girl named Tay who lived happily with her parents. Her parents were kind-hearted people who always lent a helping hand to everyone in their community. They were known for their generosity, always willing to share what they had to bring a smile to someone's face.

However, there was a challenge in Tay's family. Despite their kindness, Tay's parents struggled financially. Her mother, Sandra, worked tirelessly as a caretaker at the school, beloved by all the children for her kindness and helpfulness. Meanwhile, Tay's father, Paul, worked as a mechanic, often returning home with tired hands stained with oil from fixing cars all day.

Even though Tay's parents had jobs, they didn't earn enough for the rent. Tay heard them worried in the next room.

"We might lose our house" her mom said.

Tay's dad sighed "And I might lose my car."

Their car was old and noisy, and kids at school used to laugh at it. But they needed it to get Tay and her mom to school, as it was quite far, and Tay's dad, Paul, had to get to work.

When Tay heard her parents talking about losing everything, she quietly cried in her room because she didn't want them to know she heard it. She often heard them praying for help, hoping for a miracle.

Tay's favourite time was on Saturday mornings, when her mom, Sandra, took her shopping for groceries. They went to the cheap market, where her mom found good deals from the meat and fish man. Tay loved going to the pound shop, a store where everything costs a pound. Her favourite part was when her mom bought a lottery ticket for one pound and picked six numbers, even though they never won. Her mom used to say they'd buy a big new house and her dad, Paul, would get a fancy sports car if they ever won. Tay always asked if she could pick six numbers too, hoping for good luck, but her mom said she was too young to play.

One day, as Tay was walking into school, she dropped the glasses that were in her hand. As she went to pick them up, she noticed something shiny and golden on the ground. As she got closer and glimpsed more thoroughly, she realised she was looking at a pound coin! She looked around to see if anyone had dropped it, but she couldn't see anybody nearby. She picked it up, put it in her pocket, and hurried to school. She was running late as her dad's car took a long time to start that morning.

When Tay entered class, she got in trouble with her teacher, Mrs. Blake.

"Late again, Tay?" Mrs. Blake sighed "That's another 30 minutes of detention."

Tay slumped in her seat, muttering to herself "But it wasn't my fault..."

Throughout the day, Tay couldn't concentrate because she had never had money of her own before and now had a gold pound coin in her pocket. She wondered what to do with it. Tay thought about telling her mom, Sandra, at playtime or her dad, Paul, when he picked them up after school, but she worried they might take it away and tell her to give it to the school.

At that very moment, Tay had a brilliant idea. As soon as the bell rang for playtime, Tay ran straight to her best friend, TigerLilly.

"Do me the biggest favour, please." Tay asked Tigerlilly

TigerLilly asked "What's wrong?"

Tay replied "Nothing; I just need to call my uncle. It's important."

TigerLilly could see the anticipation on Tay's face, so she said "Yes, Tay, anything for you, my bestie."

As TigerLilly was about to take her phone out and pass it to her, Tay said "No, not here in the playground. Let's go to the cloakroom."

Tay dialled the number, and after a few rings, the phone answered.

Tay quickly burst out "Uncle Dez, can you please pick me up after school?"

Uncle Dez asked "Why? Your dad's picking you up as usual."

Tay replied "I know, but I have something very important to tell you, and you're my favourite uncle. Please, please, please."

Uncle Dez started laughing and said "Okay, kiddo. Since you're my favourite niece, I'll call your mom and tell her I'm taking you out after school."

Tay asked "Uncle Dez, are you sure mom's going to listen?"

"Of course she will listen." Uncle Dez chuckled and said "After all, your mom is my little sister."

Tay said "Thanks, Unc" blew a kiss, and put the phone down.

Tay sat in her last three lessons, eagerly waiting for the bell to ring at the end of school. When the bell finally rang.

Tay's teacher said "Tay, I just got a message from your mom. She said you must go home with your uncle. He's outside, so be careful. She loves you and will see you later."

Tay jumped up and punched the air, screaming "Yes!" with joy.

Tay ran outside and saw her uncle Dez sitting in his black BMW car, which she loved. She opened the door and jumped into the passenger seat.

Tay then said "Thank you so much, Uncle Dez, for picking me up" giving him a big kiss on the cheek.

Uncle Dez said "Alright, alright, tell me what's up, baby girl."

Tay blurted out "I found a pound outside school" and waited for Uncle Dez's reaction.

After a moment, Uncle Dez started laughing, saying "You called me to come all the way here because you found a pound on the floor?"

Tay replied "Not everyone's rich like you, Uncle Dez."

Uncle Dez chuckled "I wish I was rich."

Tay said "I want you to take me to the pound shop."

"What for?" Uncle Dez replied.

Tay said "I want you to buy me a lottery ticket. My mom puts the lottery on once a month, and I've been telling her to let me try. Mom won't listen, saying I'm too young."

Uncle Dez replied "You are too young, kiddo."

Tay insisted "I know, but that's why I want you to buy the ticket."

Uncle Dez asked "And what makes you think your lottery ticket's going to be anything special?"

Tay replied confidently "I have had six numbers written down for about a year now. It's my date of birth, and I just got this feeling inside me that they are something special."

Uncle Dez said "Okay, I will take you to the shop. I believe if you feel strongly about something, you should go for it."

"Thanks, and I heard my dad say in life that you should take risks if you want to progress, but he doesn't like taking risks." Tay explains "Right now, Uncle Dez, I'm ready to take that risk."

Uncle Dez smiled and said "Let's go."

And so they went to the pound shop. Uncle Dez purchased the lottery ticket with Tay's pound and got back into the car.

"Here you go" Uncle Dez said, handing Tay the ticket while singing the song from Willy Wonka and the Chocolate Factory "I've got a golden ticket" and laughing. Tay excitedly filled in her six numbers. Uncle Dez went back to the shop and got the receipt for the ticket with the numbers on it.

They drove to Tay's house and pulled up.

Uncle Dez said "If you win, I want half."

Tay replied "Uncle Dezzzzz, I'm doing this for one reason only: to get me and my parents out of debt and poverty and live better, like how my friend Tigerlilly lives. She has a big house and everything is brand new."

Uncle Dez chuckled "I'm only joking. Go inside, tell your mom I said hello, and make sure you pray. God hears all prayers. Remember, he loves us."

"Yes, Uncle Dez" replied Tay, and she ran into the house.

Tay's mom asked "Are you alright, baby?"

"Yes, Mom" Tay replied.

"Why did Uncle Dez want to talk to you?" asked Sandra.

"Just to give me advice about life." Tay responded.

"That sounds like your Uncle Dez, always trying to show people the right way. Anyway, dinner's in the oven. Then brush your teeth, get washed, and go to bed. School in the morning, early to bed, early to rise." Sandra stated.

"Yes, Mom. I love you, and goodnight. Tell Dad 'night-night' from me when he comes in, please." Tay pleaded.

The week went by slowly, and Tay couldn't wait until Saturday, when the national lottery came on TV, to see if she had the winning numbers. She told her Uncle Dez to hold the ticket as she had the numbers in her school bag.

Saturday came, and Tay and her mom went shopping. They came back home, and then Tay's cousins came around. Before she knew it, it was time to go to bed. While in her sleep, Tay heard her mom calling her. She woke up, rubbed her eyes and looked at the time on her dressing table. It was Sunday morning, 8 o'clock. Wondering why her mom was calling her so early.

Tay shouted back "Yes, Mom."

"Your Uncle Dez is on the phone." Tay's mom said.

Tay thought to herself about the lottery and quickly ran downstairs as fast as she could then took the phone from her mom.

"Meet me outside in 20 minutes." Said Uncle Dez over the phone

21

Tay put some music on in her bedroom but turned it down low so her mom wouldn't start complaining. She brushed her teeth, had a quick wash, sat down on her bed, and couldn't think straight as there were a million things running through her mind.

Nineteen minutes later, she was on her front lawn, anxiously waiting until she saw her uncle Dez's black BMW coming around the corner. He pulled up and she jumped in.

Tay said "My heart's racing, Uncle Dez. Why are you up so early? It's not like you."

Uncle Dez started laughing hysterically and asked "Guess what?"

Tay said "Uncle Dez, stop playing with me. Please tell me what's going on. I can't take it anymore."

"You won the lottery!" he exclaimed.

Tay tilted her head back, and it hit the back of the leather headrest. Suddenly, she became dizzy and fainted, slouching in her chair. When she opened her eyes, her uncle Dez was shaking her by her shoulders.

"I thought you'd never wake up!" he exclaimed with his loud, distinctive laugh. "Drink this" he said, handing her a cold bottle of water.

Tay took a sip and said "I needed that, thanks Uncle."

Uncle Dez smiled widely "All your six numbers came up, little girl! You're the smartest and luckiest nine-year-old I've ever known."

"Oh my God. Thanks so much, Unc!" Tay said elatedly.

"£1,000,000" Uncle Dez said, his eyes widening.

"Wow," Tay exclaimed, "what are we going to do now? I only wanted to get my parents out of debt and get some new clothes instead of wearing all my older cousin's hand-me-downs."

Uncle Dez chuckled "Oh kiddo, with this amount of money, you can do much more than that. Leave it with me."

"Alright, Uncle Dez." Tay nodded, planting a kiss on his cheek "Don't forget us."

"How can I forget you?" Uncle Dez chuckled back. "Tay, listen to me seriously. Don't tell a soul about this, not even your parents. I'll sort it out. It's our secret."

"Okay, Uncle Dez" Tay agreed "I trust you." With that, she turned and ran into the house.

Weeks passed, but Tay didn't hear from Uncle Dez. She tried calling many times, but there was no answer. Tay felt restless and couldn't sleep, wondering what was happening. Then, a month later, on a Saturday afternoon, Tay's mom told her to get ready and wear her best outfit. Tay asked where they were going, but her mom just said Uncle Dez had invited them to a meal in the suburbs and told her not to be late.

Tay didn't hesitate and thought to herself about the lottery. She dashed upstairs, washed, dressed, and hurried back down.

"Mom, I'm ready," she announced.

"I've never seen you move so fast" Tay's mom chuckled "Let's go."

During the drive, it felt like time was dragging on forever for Tay. She couldn't think straight, feeling sick with butterflies in her stomach.

When they finally arrived, all Tay could see was her Uncle Dez standing in front of his BMW car. As Tay opened the car door on that hot summer day, she was greeted by the sight of fresh green grass in a beautiful area.

Uncle Dez came over, picked up Tay, and said to Tay's parents "I've got the biggest surprise of your life."

Tay's dad, Paul, asked "What surprise is this?"

Uncle Dez replied, "The surprise is that Tay asked me to put the lottery on, gave me six numbers, and her ticket won!"

Tay's mom, Sandra, exclaimed "What?"

Uncle Dez said "Look behind me."

When they all looked past the BMW, they saw a big white mansion and a lime-green Lamborghini.

"Wow!" they all exclaimed at the same time.

Uncle Dez continued "Yes, you better thank God for your good blessings. That's all yours, all paid for, and you have half a million pounds in your bank account too. You will never have to struggle or work again."

And so, they all ran as fast as they could to their new home because it was the best day of their lives and they could finally see a bright future